LOOK AND FIND®

DREAMWORKS®

SHREK
FOREVER AFTER

To: MADISON
FROM: NANA
XMAS 2014

Illustrated by Jason Beene
Layouts by Art Mawhinney

Published by
Louis Weber, C.E.O., Publications International, Ltd.
7373 North Cicero Avenue, Lincolnwood, Illinois 60712

Ground Floor, 59 Gloucester Place, London W1U 8JJ

Customer Service: 1-800-595-8484 or customer_service@pilbooks.com

www.pilbooks.com

p i kids is a registered trademark of Publications International, Ltd.

Look and Find is a registered trademark of Publications International, Ltd., in the United States and in Canada.

8 7 6 5 4 3 2 1

ISBN-13: 978-1-60553-115-1
ISBN-10: 1-60553-115-4

pi kids® publications international, ltd.

For Shrek, every day is the same. There is always a diaper to be changed, a baby to be fed, and an outhouse to unclog. He longs for a little peace and quiet. Look through the chaos and find these signs of the family's routine.

This laundry basket

This baby bottle

These diapers

This newspaper

Sir Squeakles

This stack of dishes

It's the triplets' birthday party, and Shrek is picking up the birthday cake. But everywhere he goes is another fan. No one is afraid of ogres anymore! When the three pigs eat the cake, Shrek storms off. Can you find these goodies that the three little pigs have yet to eat?

Chocolate-chip cookies

Fudge brownies

Frosted cupcake

Gingerbread house

Jar of lollipops

Candy apples

Box of chocolates

Strawberry shortcake

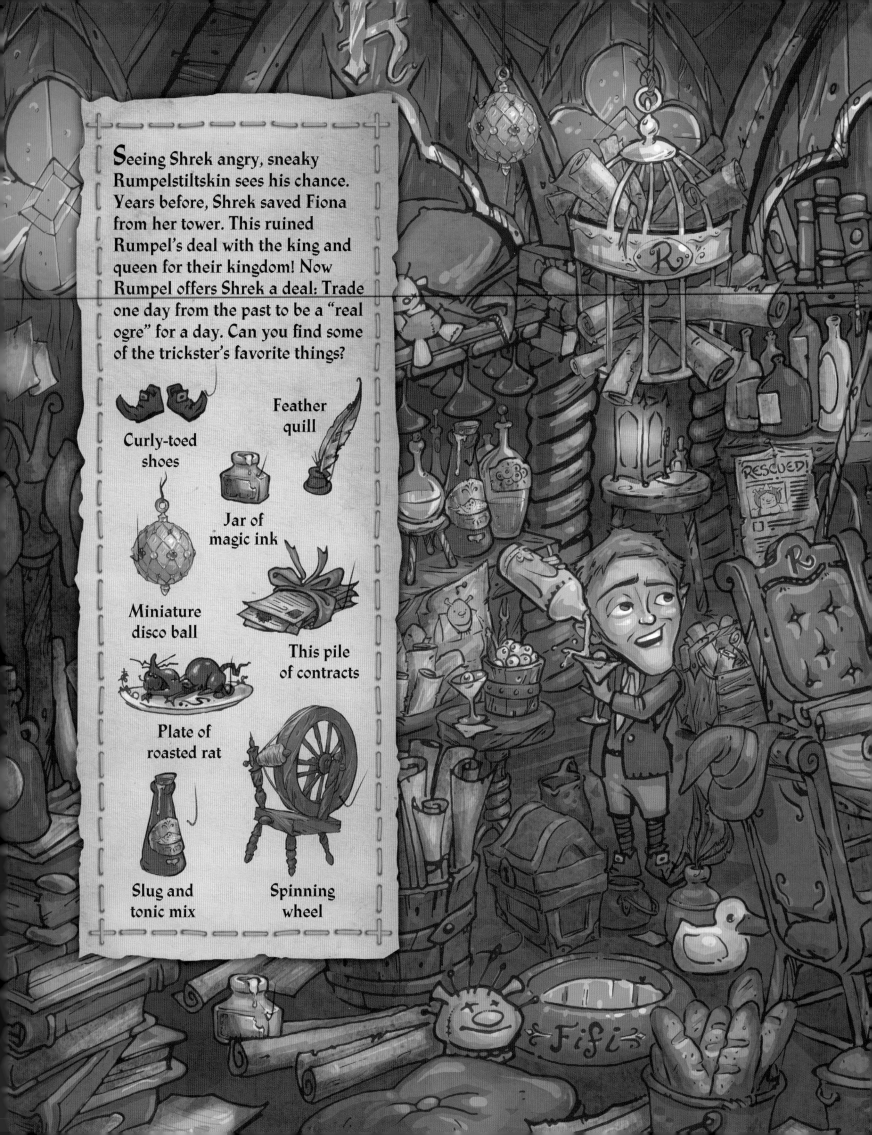

Seeing Shrek angry, sneaky Rumpelstiltskin sees his chance. Years before, Shrek saved Fiona from her tower. This ruined Rumpel's deal with the king and queen for their kingdom! Now Rumpel offers Shrek a deal: Trade one day from the past to be a "real ogre" for a day. Can you find some of the trickster's favorite things?

Curly-toed shoes

Feather quill

Jar of magic ink

Miniature disco ball

This pile of contracts

Plate of roasted rat

Slug and tonic mix

Spinning wheel

Shrek gets his wish: He is feared again. But when he sees a wanted poster for Fiona, Shrek knows something is wrong. Before he can figure it out, a witch squad captures him. Rumpel now rules the land and things are very different.

Can you find these things that have changed in Far Far Away?

Muffin Man

Donkey

Far Far Away sign

Gingy

Pinocchio

Rumpel's palace

Shrek is brought into Rumpel's palace. There, he finds out that the day Rumpel took was the day Shrek was born. That means he never met Fiona and their children were never born! Shrek manages to break free, steal a witch's broom, and grab Donkey. Can you spot who was there for the escape?

Fifi

Rumpel

Pinocchio

Jester

Amber

Big Bad Wolf

Georgette

Shrek and Donkey come across an ogre resistance camp, led by Fiona! Shrek knows that his deal with Rumpel can end through True Love's Kiss. But Fiona and the newly plump Puss don't remember him. Find these ogres and items useful to the resistance.

This map

Model of Rumpel's palace

This spear

This stuffed witch dummy

Guarding ogre

Climbing ogre

Club-carrying ogre

Cheering ogre

Rumpel captures Shrek and Fiona and holds them in his dungeon. But when they defeat Dragon and the ogre army arrives for a rescue mission, Rumpel tries to escape. Can you find him, as well as some others joining in the fight?

Rumpel

This falling witch

Cookie

Donkey

Puss

Brogan

The ogres manage to defeat Rumpel and the witches. Just as the day ends, Fiona and Shrek share True Love's Kiss. Shrek swirls back to his old life, finding himself at the triplets' birthday party. Find these friends and family members taking part in the birthday celebration.

Fergus

Farkle

Queen Lillian

Gingy

Felicia

Big Bad Wolf

Three Blind Mice

Pinocchio

Shrek loves his family, but he misses the way things used to be, too. Go back to the family's home and find these snapshots from the past.

Picture of villagers with pitchforks

Picture of Artie

Picture of the fairytale gang

Wedding portrait

Picture of the triplets as newborns

Old picture of Lillian and Harold

Shrek just can't get a moment of peace. Go back to the bakery and find these villagers and fairytale creatures who no longer fear the ogre.

Butter Pants

Little Jack Horner

Lemke

Rumpelstiltskin

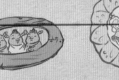
Puss

Gingy

The three pigs

Rumpelstiltskin is secretly plotting against Shrek. Go back to Rumpel's carriage and find these clues that he has a grudge against the ogre.

Ogre-shaped dartboard

Ogre-shaped pincushion

Map of Far Far Away

"No-Shrek" sign

Model of Fiona's tower

Newspaper clipping about Fiona's rescue

Things have changed a lot in Rumpel's Far Far Away. Go back and see if you can find these items.

4 banana peels

5 animal crackers

6 broken windows

7 wanted posters

8 peasant children

9 tree stumps

As Shrek and Donkey make their escape, check out Rumpel's palace for these extravagant items.

 Crown

 Jeweled curly-toed shoes

 Spool of golden thread

 Diamond-crusted cocktail shaker

 Enormous throne

 Gold statue of Rumpel

 Jeweled wig

 Candelabra

In a world without Shrek, Puss became a fat cat! Go back to the ogre camp and find these things belonging to the now-frilly kitty.

 Toy mouse

 Heart-shaped pillow

 Kitty condo

 Fancy mirror

 Jug of milk

 Fluffy cat bed

The battle at Rumpel's palace caused a lot of destruction. Go back to the throne room and find these things that were broken or tossed aside in the chaos.

 Fifi's cage

 Bookcase of contracts

 Vase

 Rumpel's wig cart

 Lamp

 Goblet

 Banquet table

Ogres have different taste when it comes to party food. Go back to the triplets' birthday party and find these not-so-tasty ogre treats.

 Eyeball salad

 Moldy cheese

 Mud cake

 Grub dip with bark chips

 Box of slug treats

 Squirmin' worms casserole